29087482

10/02

MOVING DAY

by ROBERT KALAN
pictures by YOSSI ABOLAFIA

Greenwillow Books, New York

Library of Congress Cataloging-in-Publication Data
Kalan, Robert.
Moving day / by Robert Kalan ; pictures by Yossi Abolafia.
p.   cm.
Summary: A hermit crab looking for a new home tries several
different shells before finding one that fits just right.
ISBN 0-688-13948-5 (trade).   ISBN 0-688-13949-3 (lib. bdg.)
[1. Hermit crabs—Fiction.   2. Crabs—Fiction.
3. Shells—Fiction.   4. Dwellings—Fiction.
5. Stories in rhyme.]   I. Abolafia, Yossi, ill.   II. Title.
PZ8.3.K12466Mo   1996   [E]—dc20
95-2257   CIP   AC

Hermit crabs are the recyclers of the crab family. Other crabs
protect themselves by growing their own shells. Hermit crabs
hide their soft bodies by crawling into the empty shells of
dead sea snails and other shellfish. With its body tucked deep
inside the shell, the hermit crab defends itself by holding its
large pincer across the entry. When it gets too big for its
shell, the hermit crab must find and move into a larger shell.

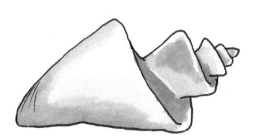

For John and Delores,
our touchstones
—R. K.

For Abe Reuben
—Y. A.

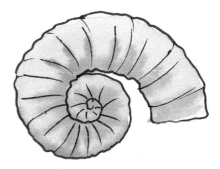

This shell is snug.
This shell is tight.

I will find a shell
that's right.

This shell is too big.

This shell is too small.

Too big,
too small,

these shells
will not do at all.

This shell is too long.

This shell is too wide.

Too long,
too wide,
too big,
too small,

these shells
will not do at all.

This shell is too heavy.

This shell is too light.

Too heavy, too light,
too long, too wide,
too big, too small,

these shells
will not do at all.

This shell is too rough.

This shell is too smooth.

Too rough, too smooth,
too heavy, too light,
too long, too wide,
too big, too small,

these shells
will not do at all.

This shell is too fancy.

This shell is too plain.

Too fancy,

 too plain,

too rough,

 too smooth,

too heavy,

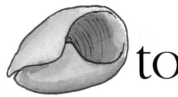 too light,

too long,

too wide,

too big,

too small,

these shells
will not do at all.

This shell is too—

Wait!

It's NOT too snug.
It's NOT too tight.
This shell is
the one that's right.

This shell has
more room inside.
Room to grow,
room to hide.

I know why
this shell is fine.
It's like that other
shell of mine.